KT-491-420

Ball

Written by
Allan Ahlberg

illustrated by
Sébastien Braun

Not eating an ice-cream or riding a bike. NO — kicking a ball is what I like.

Cumbria Libraries

3 8003 04491 6450

What I like best
Yes, most of all
In my whole life
Is . . .

Kicking a

FOR ROSS • DANIEL • NATHAN • NATHANAEL • OSH •
ROWAN • LUCAS • RONAN • LEO • BELLA ! S !

PUFFIN BOOKS
Published by the Penguin Group: London,
New York, Australia, Canada, India, Ireland,
New Zealand and South Africa
Penguin Books Ltd, Registered Offices:
80 Strand, London WC2R 0RL, England
puffinbooks.com
First published in *Heard it in the Playground*
by Viking Kestrel 1989
Revised and abridged for this edition 2014
001
Text copyright © Allan Ahlberg, 1989, 2014
Illustrations copyright © Sébastien Braun, 2014
All rights reserved
The moral right of the author and illustrator
has been asserted
Made and printed in China
ISBN: 978-0-723-27120-8

10

FOOTbALL

LIBRARY SERVICES
FOR SCHOOLS

38003044916450	
Bertrams	13/05/2014
	£6.99
LSS	

the CAFÉ

LETTERS

NOt reading a book or writing a letter.

NO – kicking a ball is TWENTY times better!

Not PUNCHING a ball

Or BASHING a ball

SERVING a ball

Or SMASHING a ball

Not THROWING a ball

Or BLOWING a ball

Not BOWLING or BATTING

Or PATTING a ball

Not PINGING or PONGING

Or POTTING or PUTTING

BUT BOOTING and SHOOTING

SCRATCHHH!

a BALL.

A BALL in the playground .... A BALL on the grass ....

A BALL before breakfast .... A BALL before bed ....

----- A SHOT on the run ----------- A DRIBBLE, a PASS.

----- A dream of a BALL ------------- A 'GOAL' in the head.

Don't want a ball
That's **ODD** or *screw*
That you hit with a mallet
Or a billiard cue.

Don't want a ball
That's made of meat
I'd really rather
SCORE than eat!

NOT a ballcock

REFILL TUBE — FLOAT

TRIP LEVER

LIFT STRAP

TILT VALVE

PINION HOLDER

BALLCOCK

OR a ballpoint

Scapula

Humerus

OR a plastic ball-and-socket joint.

NOT a ball bearing
(bit too small)

BUT — putting it more or less
baldly —

?

A BALL.

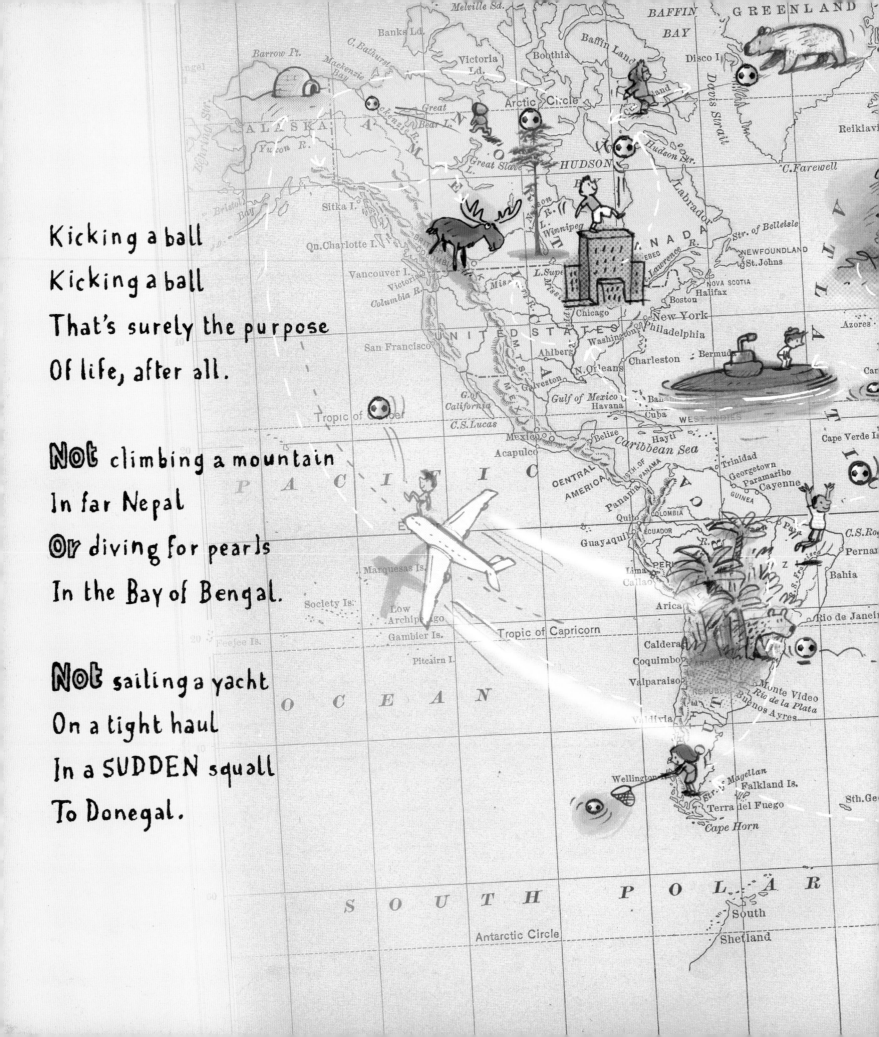

Kicking a ball
Kicking a ball
That's surely the purpose
Of life, after all.

Not climbing a mountain
In far Nepal
Or diving for pearls
In the Bay of Bengal.

Not sailing a yacht
On a tight haul
In a SUDDEN squall
To Donegal.

But kicking a ball

Kicking a ball

kick,

kick,

Kick, kick, kicking a BALL!

And later on
As the years pass
I'll still be running
Across the grass.

Kicking a ball
Kicking a ball
With Clive and Malcolm
Trevor and Paul.

Reading the paper, having a shave
Forcing the 'goalie' to make a save.

Kissing my wife, bathing our baby
Kicking a ball and SCORING (maybe).

Till baby toddles
And **tackles** and then ...

Starts the ball rolling
All over again.

What I like best, yes, most of all in my **whole life**, is kicking a ball.

In freezing cold ------------ or blinding heat ------------

Caked in mud ------------ covered in sweat ------------

EVER and ALWAYS, a ball at my feet.

SCORING the GOALS I'll never forget.

Yes, life's a circle, endless and SMALL

And when all's said and done...

...the world's a BALL.